Wind

By Ron Bacon

Illustrated by Philippa Stichbury

READ BY READING Series

Ashton Scholastic

Auckland   Sydney   New York   London   Toronto

Feel the wind blowing by,

lifting kites up to the sky.

3

Feel the wind blowing through,

chasing clouds across the blue.

Feel the wind blowing free,

stirring white caps on the sea

Feel the wind blowing fast,

whipping sand and papers past.

Feel the wind blowing strong!

tossing leaves and grass along.

Feel the wind blowing hard,

flinging rubbish round the yard.

Feel the wind blowing on

soft, then softer, till it's gone.